Molly
and the
Beanstalk

Molly
and the
Beanstalk

Pippa Goodhart
Illustrated by Brita Granström

WALKER
BOOKS

For all the children at
Overdale Infant School in Leicester
P.G.

First published 2001 by Walker Books Ltd
87 Vauxhall Walk, London SE11 5HJ

Sprinters edition published in hardback by Heinemann Library,
a division of Reed Educational and Professional Publishing Limited,
by arrangement with Walker Books Ltd

This edition published 2017

2 4 6 8 10 9 7 5 3 1

Text © 2001 Pippa Goodhart
Illustrations © 2001 Brita Granström

The right of Pippa Goodhart and Brita Granström to be identified as author
and illustrator respectively of this work has been asserted by them
in accordance with the Copyright, Designs and Patents Act 1988

This book has been typeset in Garamond

Printed in Great Britain by Clays Ltd, St Ives plc

British Library Cataloguing in Publication Data:
a catalogue record for this book is available from the British Library

ISBN 978-1-4063-7878-8

www.walker.co.uk

Contents

Chapter One

Molly and Old Ma Coddle lived on a little farm with Sylvie Cow, some hens and a few ducks on a pond.

Molly would look over the fence
to the world beyond and wonder,
What would it be like to see new
places and meet new people?

Molly knew that there was more in the world than the world she knew because Old Ma told her stories. She told stories about giants and magic and much more.

It was spring. Old Ma and Molly
seeded and weeded and sowed
and hoed.

"I wish I could sow a story seed," said Molly.

"Well, wishes are a kind of seed," said Old Ma.

"So, am I sowing a seed just by wishing?"

"Maybe you are," said Old Ma. "Look at the sky, Molly. I think a story *might* just be starting. The clouds are melting away. Something strange is happening to the weather."

Chapter Two

Day after day, the sun shone in the sky, hotter and hotter. The seeds began to sprout, but their green stems soon shrivelled as the earth baked dry.

Sylvie Cow's tail swung to swat away the flies as she stood in the shade and chewed on the few blades of grass she could find. Molly leaned against her soft side. "Oh, it's hot, hot, hot," she said.

Molly and Old Ma struggled from the pond to the fields with buckets of water. But even the pond was drying out and the ducks had flown away.

"This is horrible," said Molly. "If this is part of my story, I don't like it."

Old Ma mopped her face with a flap of apron. "But Molly," she said, "most stories have to start with a bad bit. If they didn't, then how could things get better and end happily?"

Molly's story got worse. The sun shone hotter and Sylvie Cow got thinner and thinner. There was no milk, no butter, no cheese. Old Ma got thinner too. She got ill.

There were no vegetables and
no fruit and the hungry hens had
stopped laying eggs.

"We'll starve!" said Molly.

"You must go and sell some of our things," said Old Ma. "We need money to buy food if we can't grow it ourselves."

So Molly put on her sunhat and walked to market with a wheelbarrow full of plates and jugs and pictures.

She sold them all for a fistful of coins. Then she used the money to buy bread and cheese and honey and a small bundle of hay. She walked wearily home.

"At least we won't be hungry now," Molly told Sylvie Cow as she fed her the hay. "And perhaps my story will start to get better."

Chapter Three

But in a few days they had eaten
all the bread and cheese and honey
and hay. More days passed and still
the sun shone hot and no rain fell.
Sylvie Cow's ribs showed. Molly was
thin too.

Old Ma just stayed in bed, and that frightened Molly.

"What do I do now, Old Ma?" asked Molly. "I don't want this story any more. Can't we just stop it and go back to normal?"

But Old Ma shook her poor tired head. "You can't stop a story once it's started," she said. "A story isn't a story unless it has a beginning and a middle and an end."

Molly sighed. "But what can I do to hurry it on to a better bit?"

"You must sell Sylvie Cow," said Old Ma.

"Oh no!" said Molly. "I love Sylvie Cow."

"I do too, Molly, but Sylvie Cow is all we have left."

25

So Molly slipped a rope around
Sylvie's curly horns, and she led her
to the market in town.

Chapter Four

The butcher in town looked at
Sylvie Cow and offered Molly shiny
coins. But Molly saw the butcher's
shiny sharp knife, and she turned
and ran with Sylvie Cow, away and
away and up into green hills.

Molly told Sylvie Cow, "I wish we could stay here in the hills.

There's all the grass that you could ever eat and I'm sure there's food for people too." But Molly remembered poor Old Ma, ill and hungry at home. "I can't stay," she said. "And if I leave you here, who will look after you?"

Molly looked up and saw a boy in a tree.

"Who are you?" she asked.

"I'm Jack," said the boy. "I'd give your cow the best grass and I'd milk her every morning and evening."

"Would you talk to her too?"
asked Molly.

"I would," said Jack. "I have
nobody else to talk to."

"I have," said Molly. "I've got
Old Ma at home. But the weather
has gone wrong and nothing will
grow and we have nothing to eat.

If you bought Sylvie Cow, then I could buy food for Old Ma and me."

But Jack shook his head. "I can't buy your cow. I have no money. Look!" He jumped down from the tree and pulled his pockets inside out. All that came out was one bean.

Molly looked at the lush green grass all around. She looked at poor Sylvie's tired drooping head. She looked at Jack's kind eyes – and she decided.

"You can have Sylvie Cow if you give me the bean. Just so long as you love her and give her back to me when the weather comes right."

 So Molly hugged Sylvie Cow's bony neck and promised to have her home soon. Then she left her with Jack.

Molly ran all the way back to her hot bare home where the sun still shone and Old Ma was still ill in bed.

Chapter Five

Molly told Old Ma about the lush green grass in the hills. "I left Sylvie Cow with Jack. They will be happy."

"And what did this Jack boy pay for the cow?" asked Old Ma.

Molly showed her the bean.

"One mean little bean!" shouted Old Ma, sitting up in bed. "You gave away our Sylvie Cow for one hard little bean? Oh Molly!" And Old Ma wobbled up from her bed and went to the window and threw the bean out.

Molly began to
cry, and she ran
outside, away
from cross Old
Ma. She found
the bean on the
ground. She knelt

down beside it and she cried with
hunger and hurt. She sobbed, "Oh,
I don't want to be in this story any
more! Please make it stop!"

What Molly didn't see was that
her tears watered the earth, and the
bean began to grow.

What Molly didn't know was
that her story had got to its middle.
Things were about to change.

Chapter Six

Molly lay in bed, too unhappy
and hungry to sleep. She thought
about the bean. Perhaps she could
clean it and nibble it and fill a
little of her hungry tummy?

So she lit a lantern and went searching the dark for the purple dot of bean.

She looked on the ground, but what she found made her tip back her head and look up, up and up.

"WOW!"
said Molly.
"A beanstalk
that's bigger
than a tree!"
And Molly
thought of
the enormous
beans that
must grow
somewhere at
the top of
that stalk.

Molly put the lantern between
her teeth, and she began to climb.
Up and up and up until ...

a dazzle of bright light made her
drop the lantern in surprise and
cover her eyes.

Molly saw giant orange flowers
and giant green beans. Then she
saw something else; something that
moved. She looked up and up again
and saw...

Chapter Seven

"A GIANT!" said Molly.

"No," said the giant. "I'm just a girl. My name is Molly. But *what* and *who* are you?"

"I'm Molly too," said Molly. "I live down there on the farm," and she pointed.

The giant Molly bent down close
and poked little Molly with one
finger. "Are you real?" she asked.

"Of course I am!" said Molly.
"I must be, because I'm hungry!
And so is Old Ma. It's been hot,
hot, hot and our plants have
died and Sylvie Cow has gone.

We're starving. But one of your big beans could feed us for a week. Please, could I take one?"

"I don't think you can," said the giant Molly. "They're just the pattern on my bed cover."

She picked up giant pens and
paper and scissors, and she drew
and she cut and she gave Molly
some beans so big she had to
hug them.

"Thank you!" said Molly. "You are kind."

"Well, I want to help you," said the giant Molly.

"I think that your weather going wrong might have been my fault," she continued. "I've been hot, hot, hot with a fever. But I think I'm better now. Maybe that means things will get better for you too?"

 "Oh yes!" Molly pointed. "Look down there! There are clouds again. It's raining! Everything will grow again now. I think my story must be getting near the end. Please, could you put everything back as it should be?"

Chapter Eight

Next morning the giant Molly
picked up Sylvie Cow and Jack and
she put them back at the farm.

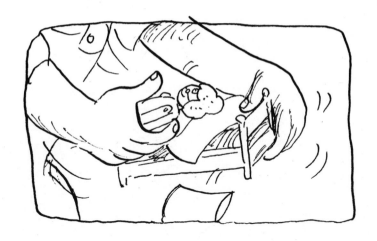

She took Old Ma from her bed
and put her in the doorway.

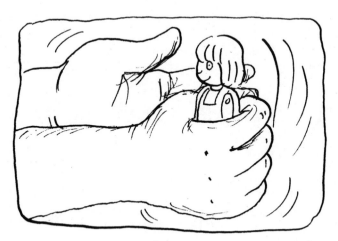

And, very gently, she put Molly
back on the ground.

Chapter Nine

The rain made everything fresh
and green again. Old Ma and Molly
made bean soup and bean salad,
bean fritters and bean cake, and
they decorated the farm with giant
orange bean flowers.

Jack milked Sylvie Cow

and he
skimmed cream

and
slapped butter

and pressed cheese.

When their feast was ready, they
sang and they danced and they ate
and they drank.

Then they were tired and it was time to sit and tell stories.

Jack told the first one. It was a sad story of how he came to have no home and no family.

Then Molly said, "Why don't you stay and live with us? You could be my brother and Old Ma could be your granny."

"I'd like that, Jack," said Old Ma.

"So would I," said Jack, and he smiled.

Then Molly told a story called *Molly and the Beanstalk*.

"Does it end with 'they all lived happily ever after'?" asked Old Ma.

It does!

And they did.

Pippa Goodhart has written many other books for young and older readers, including *Glog*, *Toffee and Pie*, *Flow*, shortlisted for the Smarties Prize, and *Ginny's Egg*, shortlisted for the Young Telegraph Book of the Year. However, Pippa has not always known she wanted to be a writer. She says of her school years, "I was slow to learn to read (I can still remember the agony) and so poor at spelling that I thought I was bad at writing." She did not let her early experiences put her off, however, and worked for several years in bookshops before becoming a full-time writer. She now lives in Leicester with her husband Mick, an architect, and their three children.